the view from the horizon

the view from

the horizon

constructions by Timothy Drever, 1972
texts and maps by Tim Robinson, 1975-96

CORACLE 1997

introduction

THIS COLLECTION AND mutual confrontation of pre-existant works arises out of a retrospective puzzling over a juncture in my life, between the years I passed as a visual artist under the name Timothy Drever, mainly in London, and those spent first in the Aran Islands and then in Connemara as a writer and map-maker, Tim Robinson.

Whereas I used to be dismayed by the breakage and loss caused by that sudden change in habit and habitat, nowadays it is the unchipped good order in which my little store of imagery accompanied me on the jolting journey from city to island that makes me wonder if it is ever possible to step beyond oneself. The question became sharp for me recently as I approached completion of the body of texts and maps I would have claimed had been inspired by my encounter with the west of Ireland, because in trying to forsee what I might do next I mentally revisited that earlier time of change, unwrapped some artworks stored away from my last year in London before the transition date of November 1972 — and discovered in them a concentrated abstract of the suite of images that has controlled my subsequent writing and is implicit in my cartography.

The way of that transition, so far as concerns art, and leaving aside a complex of personal and practical considerations and the deep involvement of my partner M in every aspect of it, was thus. Having mounted several exhibitions of non-figurative paintings and latterly of large environmental installations, and although these had been kindly enough received by the critics, I found myself increasingly inclined to reclusion from the London art scene; indeed I felt contaminated by it. My work became an almost totally private and meditative activity, and eventually there was so little for anyone to see in it that the move from making objects to putting words into a notebook which could be shut at the end of each day was a small one, and my final disappearance to the Aran Islands hardly caused a ripple of talk in circles which perhaps once had had hopes of my career. The construction and the two assemblages illustrated here date from just before I achieved invisibility, and were seen only by a few visitors to my studio in London; since then they had lain in attics and cellars, until in that recent reminiscential moment I took them out to see if they had anything to say to me today. By coincidence, just when I was mulling over this flotsam from a previous career, came an invitation to contribute to an exhibition of European artworks, to be curated by Michael Tarantino for the Irish Museum of Modern Art. And so, with many misgivings, I decided to make the three works the core of an installation that would externalise the questioning mood they had precipitated in me.

The principal piece of the three is a slender, yard-long, white-painted wooden rod, suspended vertically from a large number of fine threads of many colours, which radiate from the centre of its upper end and are pinned almost randomly to the ceiling or the upper parts of the walls and furnishings of whatever space it is mounted in. When it inhabited the middle air of my studio I used to think of it as a pace taken towards the centre of the earth. Closely related to it is a collection of wooden rods of lengths from about three to eight feet and of thicknesses from a quarter of an inch to two inches or so, painted in black and white bands in various combinations of width. These used to lie stacked in a loose bundle in a corner or all crisscrossed on the floor in a way that reminded me of my grandmother's little set of ivory spillikins. The same sort of visual tick-tock runs through them all, but each has its own rate and rhythm, weight and balance, and I used to hand them one by one to whomever called to see them. An art-critical friend wondered if they were 'measure become organic', and indeed one might imagine them to be growth-stages in the life of a measuring-rod. There used to be two or three very big ones too, twenty or thirty feet long, which I sup-

THE INSTALLATION AT THE IRISH MUSEUM OF MODERN ART

pose rightly formed part of the assemblage but were left outside leaning up into trees and have not accompanied me down to the present. As to the third work, I have no memory of making it and was surprised when I found it bundled up with the others. It comprises thirty-five thin white wooden rods each thirty-five inches long. On each one a different inch-long segment is picked out in grey, so that if they are laid side by side in a certain order the grey inch appears to progress regularly from one end to the other, but of course this symmetry is broken when they are dropped and scattered. None of these three works had names so far as I can remember, but for present purposes I have called them, respectively, 'To the Centre', 'Auto-biography' and 'Inchworm'.

Also included in the installation were two maps, sections from which are illustrated here — that of Conn-emara, made between 1980 and 1990, and, more recent, my third and final attempt upon the cartography of the Aran Islands - together with a number of short texts, most of which derive from passages in my books *Stones of Aran* and *Setting Foot on the Shores of Connemara and Other Writings*. These excerpts were lightly reworked to wean them from their original contexts and confront them with their dependence on the same fund of imagery as the three visual works. This brings me to the question of the installation's coherence with the theme of the IMMA exhi-bition, whose title was borrowed from that of an essay by Antonioni, 'The Event Horizon'.

The idea of participating in The Event Horizon had immediately attracted me because of the close connection between the cosmological concept of that name, so awesomely deployed in conjunction with that of the black hole in Stephen Hawking's bestsellers of recent years, and that of the 'light-cone', which for me goes back at least as far as a lay person's introduction to relativity theory I read as a youth, and which is in fact the mother-image of the whole flock of metaphors I am shepherding in the installation and the present book. The matter is a little complicated but is worth teasing out further.

The three dimensions of space plus that of time cannot easily be represented together on the page, and so it is usual for diagrams in cosmology books to reduce space to two dimensions, and leave a good deal to our more or less baffled imaginations. In the diagram here the horizontal plane stands for space and the vertical dimension for time, the upwards direction being taken as that of the future. Any point in this diagram can represent an event in space-time. If the event represented by point A is the emission in all directions of a burst of radiation, the space-time diagram shows the diverging rays as constituting a cone with its vertex at A. Since nothing can travel faster than light, the career of any other signal, object or effect emanating from the event A will be represented by a line on or within the cone. Thus events lying outside the cone cannot be affected by A, being too far away from it in space for anything to reach them in time, and so the

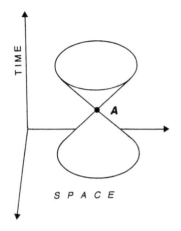

surface of the cone is the boundary between the regions of space-time that might be influenced by the event *A* and those that cannot. Similarly an inverted cone opening out from the same vertex but in the downward direction, that is, towards the past, separates all the events that could possibly have an effect upon *A* from those that could not. Immediately one sees that the light-cone is a powerful emblem of the way in which each and every event brings a certain realm of the past to a focus, and issues forth into an ever-widening future.

Since as Einstein has shown light-rays are bent by gravity, the light-cone associated with an event in the region of a large star, for instance, will be distorted by its presence; in fact its future-half will be tilted towards the star. When a giant star dies and collapses in on itself so that matter in its core is compressed to densities millions of times greater than anything in everyday experience, its gravitational field can become so powerful that all light in the vicinity is pulled into it; that is, the light-cones of events up to a certain distance from it are totally inturned towards it, so that no signal or material object can escape from it and, in the cosmologists' rather demeaning jargon, it becomes a 'black hole'. The event horizon is then the boundary within which nothing can escape engulfment.

Thus if the event horizon is a natural metaphor of the zone of the incomprehensible and unknowable attending life's rarer, more dramatic or glamorous events (which is, I take it, the sense of it that Antonioni had in mind), the light-cone can be understood as the assertion that any event, however pedestrian or mundane, is both the culmination of processes which entrain more and more of the past the further back one traces them, and the origin of an ever-widening schism between what will be, as a result of that event, and what will not. But if causality just pours through each event in this way like sand flowing without change in form or substance from one bulb of an eggtimer to the other, what do we know of choice and chance, what of creativity? If so drastic a step as abandoning a career and a home, each of them close to a sort of cultural centrality, for an unknown language, an untried art and 'a wet rock in the Atlantic' is not sufficient to shake up one's deepest vocabulary, then where is there a possibility of self-transcendence?

Of course such a vocabulary is a part of the self's structure the origins of which lie below or have sunk beneath consciousness. These images of mine, visual and textual, were not knowingly concocted but rather seemed at the time to have arise spontaneously, as 'inspiration'. Clearly the Surrealists were wrong; dreams and fantasies are not the fields of wild freedoms but of habits we don't know we have. In fact it may be that the deeper mental processes including those of artistic creation do their work without benefit or need of consciousness. But when the hidden assumptions of one's self-system are to be questioned, and, hopefully, rewritten, should consciousness then come into its own?

Hence, feeling the desire for and apparent impossibility of another mental or physical remove, I find myself engaged in the anxious self-exegesis I have represented in 'The View from the Horizon'.

Tim Robinson
Roundstone, 1997

1

A MOMENT OF stillness in the preparation of food and drink. Her firm hand supports the jug; the task enacts itself, as vision fills the passive eye.

Gravity, light, milk, bread.

The milk answers gravity most explicitly, flowing in its motionless column.
Matter is most intensely present to the senses in the bread, broken open, inviting taste, smell, touch.
But among the heavy earthenware and hanging materials the bread is a mere froth. Tempting and trapping the eye in hundreds of sparkling voids, it almost escapes the condition of weight.
Over every surface there are soft dispersions of light; it is the milk that calls them together into white, the sum of colours.

So the existence of this woman is crossed by the two pairs: milk and bread, won from life by life; gravity and light, the unconsidered sustenance we share with the inanimate. The cross marks a moment, the reflection of this moment in which you stand, watching a reflection of Vermeer's light unfold about these words, while behind the beating of your heart a pulseless gravitational heart makes itself known.

2

COSMOLOGISTS NOW SAY that Time began ten or fifteen thousand million years ago, and that the horizon of the visible universe is therefore the same number of light-years distant from us. Let this number stand as the context, the ultimate context, of my writing and your reading of these words, that arise like an inwardly directed signpost at one particular little crossroads of reality, the intersection of my life with a spell of Aran's existence.

But if it is true that Time began, it is clear that nothing else has begun since, that every apparent beginning is a stage in an elder process. The compass rose that unfurled about me in Aran, I now discover, had its stem in London.

3

I WAS ON a summer's beach one blinding day watching the waves unmake each other, when I became aware of a wave, or a recurrent sequence of waves, with a denser identity and more purposeful momentum than the rest. This appearance, which passed by from east to west and then from west to east, resolved itself under my stare into the fins and backs of two or perhaps three dolphins. I waded out until they were passing and repassing within a few yards of me, but it was still difficult to see the smoothly arching succession of dark presences as a definite number of individuals. Yet their unity with their background was no jellyfish-like dalliance with dissolution; their mode of being was an intensification of their medium into alert, reactive self-awareness; they were wave made flesh, with minds solely to ensure the moment-by-moment reintegration of body and world.

This instance of a wholeness beyond happiness made

me a little despondent, standing there thigh-deep in Panthalassa: a dolphin may be its own poem, but we have to find our rhymes elsewhere, between words in literature, between things in science, and our way back to the world involves us in an endless proliferation of detours. Let the problem be symbolized by that of taking a single step as adequate to the ground it clears as is the dolphin's arc to its wave. Is it possible to think towards a *human* conception of this 'good step'? At least, in Aran, of the world's countless facets one of the most finely carved by nature, closely structured by labour and minutely commented by tradition, I had found an exemplary terrain on which to dream of that work, the guidebook to the adequate step. And although I am aware that that moment on the beach, like all moments one remembers as creative, owes as much to the cone of futurity opening out from it as to the focusing of the past it accomplished, I take it as the site of my writing, from which to tell the heedless dolphins how it is, to walk this paradigm of broken, blessed, Pangaea.

4

BUT THE NOTION of the adequate step, a momentary con-
gruence between the culture one bears and the ground
that bears one, eventually shatters against reality into
uncountable fragments, the endless variety of steps that
are more or less good enough for one or two aspects of the
here and now. These splinters might be put together into
a more serviceable whole by paying more heed to their
cumulative nature, to the step's repeatability, variability,
reversability and expendability. The step, so mobile, so
labile, so nimbly coupling place and person, mood and
matter, occasion and purpose, begins to emerge as a
metaphor of a certain way of living on this earth. It is a
momentary proposition put by the individual to the non-
individual, an instant of trust which may not be well-
founded, a not-quite-infallible catching of oneself in the
act of falling. Stateless, the step claims a foot-long nation-
ality every second. Having endlessly variable grounds, it

needs no faith. The idea of freedom is associated in dozens of turns of phrase with that of the step. To the footloose all boundaries, whether academic or national, are mere administrative impertinences. With this free-booter's licence there goes every likelihood of superficiality, restlessness, fickleness and transgression — and so, by contraries, goes the possibility of recurrency, of frequentation, of a deep, an ever-deeper, dwelling in and on a place, a sum of whims and fancies totalling a constancy as of stone.

5

THE ROUND TOWER of Aran is fallen, and reconstructing the times it watched over is as impossible as climbing its spiral stairs of empty air. We know the names of just two of the eighth-century abbots, and mere fables about St Enda's foundation of the monastery. The majestic tower of history tapers into nothingness, leaving the the saint's earlier successors lost like stars in the daylight somewhere above the vertex of its roof, while the originary radiance behind them is as full of darkness as the empty summer sky when one stares up into it. Was there in fact a St Enda? Just as cosmologists now sense through their radio-telescopes a faint radiancy that has been batting about an expanding universe for so long that it has cooled almost, but not quite, to absolute zero, so, when I pore over the strange stories in the medieval *Vita* of the saint I feel some warmth of truth emanating from them. The crackling of the unimaginable fire out of which our galaxy, sun and earth were born is itself only a rumour of the single point from which all things sprang; from his inexistent tower the saint's bell still recalls that dawn of terrible perfection. I need this chapter of Aran's foundation-myth as reassurance that something more can always be founded on these stones. But absolute beginnings are too aflame with potentiality to contemplate with the naked eye, and only lapse of time and corruption of report makes them bearable. The abyssal upward perspective to the point of origin has to be clouded with myths and tales of false miracles, to celebrate and obscure the fact that there is only one true miracle, which itself is all-inclusive.

6

NOT FAR FROM one corner of a certain crag on Aran is —
I interrupt myself to apologize for this topographical vague-
ness, which, uncharacteristic as it is of my work, so dense
with a superfluity of distances, bearings and dimensions
specified more accurately than needful for a travellers' guide
or a literary evocation of the Aran of my memories as to suf-
fuse with space — and space of the most everyday sort, the
mere objective underlay of more subjective measures, even if
slightly humanized by my preference for inches and feet
(body-bits, fossilized, but not quite cold), yards and miles
and the human pace that guarantees them, rather than the
metric arbitrarily hinged on the meridian of Paris and the
false start of the Year One — to the point of intoxication the
consciousness that is being built up, coral-wise, by my writ-
ing towards a sense, crystallized from oceanic solutes, of the
coherence of mind with all that stems from and is still in a
connection that can be symbolized as spatial with that uni-

versal origin, the dot, the full-stop to nothingness in relation to which I stand at this moment like a fingerless finger-post at ground-zero, is an exception forced upon me by the existence, obliging me to break the continuity of my progress from east to west with this locational obfuscation, and inducing an irruption of indignation that makes me try to say everything at once, of people — my curse on them: may they wander moon-cold crags for eternity! — for whom, because they would use me as a guide to something they could break out of the continuity of Aran to steal, being so lost to a sense of where things should be that one has to deny them the knowledge of where things are, apology should be addressed to Aran itself, that stone-deaf land from which all our apostrophes re-echo, readdressed as, in this instance, the apology of the human mind to itself — a dark spiral mark on the rock-surface, that draws the eye in like a vortex...

7

A BLIND MAN from Connemara heard of a holy well on Aran, and came to see if he might be cured. Somehow he was left to find his own way to it across the crags, and while he was groping and stumbling he heard a voice calling his name. He followed the sound, and found the well, and found he could see. But he saw nobody near. The well itself had spoken.

This to me sounds like truth — truth of a mythic sort, which is strictly pragmatic, truth one can use. It proposes this well as a point from which to listen, letting the island recompose itself as speech or music. Even the muffled drumbeat of the ocean comes to it, from the caverns of Blind Sound, a mile away to the south. How appositely that placename comes in! — as if to make the point that, to the making of a point, all other points are apposite. But my sense of this truth is both foundational and precarious. I have once or twice tried walking across the fissured crag to this well with my eyes closed. Aiming to get to the well from the field-wall fifty yards east of it, I found that I could feel my way over the large crevices easily enough, but I always ended up on the sloping ground to the left of the well, no doubt because of an unmasterable, visceral, awareness of the cliff on its right. The experiment clarified the nature of a step, though. As the foot descends through space, a surface exactly the size and shape of the foot-sole receives it; this support is the top of a column of inconceivable height that goes down and down, narrower and narrower, until it rests upon a point, a nothing, at the centre of the earth, and from that point opens up again in the opposite direction like the cone of futurity opening out of a moment, into the unsoundable.

8

I IMAGINE THAT the beam of the lighthouse sweeping over the rooftops of Aran's westernmost village gives night a pulse so familiar that its cessation in dense fog must wake the households, as one is woken by a ticking clock's falling silent. And I can also feel how that cone of light, or as much of it as has failed to contact rock or ship or human eye, sails on over the horizon to drown itself in infinite space.

9

I ROVED SUNSETWARDS over the great shoulders of rock towards the western point of the island. The golden eye of the lighthouse was opening and shutting. I became elated by the vast level tide-race of sunlight streaming around me, so palpable it might have been imagined by someone blind from birth, a warm liquid pressing in at the eyes, carrying sharp exciting crystals. I began to run, exulting in the miraculous surety of my footfalls, crossing the areas chopped up by shadow-filled fissures as easily as the great burnished rock-sheets, and leaping down the scarps from terrace to terrace as if the light were dissolving them and I could plunge through them like waves.

This episode took place early in my learning about Aran; it does not represent a summation, a reading, of the work I have done since, a hard-won adequation of step to stone. Unearned, promising nothing beyond the moment of itself, least of all was it a mystic flight above or from the ground of my writing. But what could be more natural than that space should reward me for my fidelity by providing this excursus from time?

10

THE UTILITY OF a map is in its being a visual calculus for topography. In my own maps this aspect only arises incidentally and inescapably, the web of self-centred spatial relationships, which one might symbolize by the compass rose, being inextricable from the totality of directions from point to point. We could not use or even bear to look at a map that was not mostly blank. This emptiness is to be filled in with our own imagined presence, for a map is the representation, simultaneously, of a range of possible spatial relations between the map-user and a part of the world. The compass rose represents the self in these potential relationships; it is usually discreetly located in some unoccupied corner, but is conceptually transplantable to any point of the map sheet. Its meagre petals are a conventional selection of the transfinity of directions radiating from the self to the terrain. It is a skeletal flower, befitting our starved spatial consciousness. For our existence hardly knows that it is at all times wrapped in the web of directions and distances constituting space — inescapable and all-sustaining space, our unrecognized god.

This irreducible nub of topographicity is my emblem as map maker. I present the exiguous mystic bloom of the compass rose to the one who unfolds my map and finds herself a point upon it. It comes from 'a god unrecognised, a ghost denied, a lost friend, a self to whom you had died'. Alternatively it comes from something as crashingly obvious as an Ox, and I, imitating the Rosenkavalier, have cheekily appropriated it for my own wooing of the world's wide spaces.

11

PAUSING TO CATCH my breath near the top of a mountain in Connemara, I turned to look across the plain that stretches southwards and breaks up into islands scattering out into the Atlantic. A few miles away an isolated hill arose out of these lowlands, a dark pyramid against the light-flooded distances. I noticed that, from where I stood, the top of it was exactly level with the ocean horizon. That meant that a straight line drawn from my eye to the summit of that hill would go on to graze the curve of the Earth's surface, like a tangent to a circle. Surely, I thought, I could calculate the radius of the Earth from this observation. In fact by taking angular observations, from where I was now and from the top of the hill, of either end of a straight stretch of the coast-road visible below, and then going down and pacing out its length, I could arrive at a crude estimate of the size of the Earth in terms of my own stride, without recourse to astronomy, the compass, or even a map.

One reason this might seem significant to me is that for over twenty years now I have been exploring with manic attention a rather limited patch of that globe — and if the countless footsteps I have taken in this terrain have not in some sense carried me beyond its horizon, then I have cast away a large proportion of my life.

12

THIS IMAGERY OF steps, walks, mazes, webs, is not entirely something I have freely chosen to elaborate, and it could become a knot-garden I have to cut my way out of. Perhaps I need to quit these worn ways and trodden shores, to test these ideas elsewhere, to travel in search of that impossibility, the view from the horizon. I know that the step, for instance, is not some poetic flower casually picked by the wayside of my west-of-Ireland life, because, looking back, I see it implicit in the work I was doing in London, such as the yard-long suspended rod, which now rhymes mysteriously with my trigonometric musings on the Connemara mountain.

Clearly, then, a devotion to steps was something I carried with me on that decisive step from city to island. Indeed a related image comes back to me from much earlier days. I must have been eight or nine—old enough anyway to have learned that the earth spins in space, and seemingly to have picked up Newton's Law that action and reaction are equal and opposite — when it occurred to me one day that it is the effect of all the people walking on it that makes the globe turn. I soon realized, of course, that the net outcome of those multitudinous tiny impulses in all directions would be zero. That was my rational mind forming itself, by closing itself. Now I can open it again to that image of the world's endless random turnings under the feet of its inhabitants.

Since it seems that such thoughts came with me to these western corners, perhaps I do not need to go beyond present horizons to test them further. Perhaps I will not travel. But mentally I am already turning the globe, this way, that way.

The texts derive from the following writings:

1. an unpublished note on Vermeer's 'The Milkmaid', c. 1971.
2, 3. 'Timescape with Signpost', *Stones of Aran: Pilgrimage* (Lilliput Press 1986, Penguin Books 1990).
4. 'The Step', *Pilgrimage*.
5. 'The Invisible Tower' and 'Origin and Vanishing-Point', *Stones of Aran: Labyrinth* (Lilliput Press 1995, Penguin Books 1997).
6. 'The Clock', *Labyrinth*.
7. 'An Unfathomable Puddle', *Labyrinth*.
8, 9. 'Running out of Time', *Labyrinth*.
10. 'On the Cultivation of the Compass Rose' (written 1973), in *Setting Foot on the Shores of Connemara and Other Writings* (Lilliput Press 1996).
11, 12. 'Taking Steps' (originally a 'Letter from Ireland', BBC 1996), in *Setting Foot &c.*

The maps are excerpted from *Connemara: Part 1, a One-inch Map; Part 2, Introduction and Gazetteer* (Folding Landscapes 1990), and *Oileáin Árann, a Map of the Aran Islands, and a Companion to the Map* (Folding Landscapes 1996).

BRONZE-AGE STANDING STONES ALIGNED ON THE
SETTING SUN, MIDWINTER'S DAY, CONNEMARA

AN EXCERPT FROM THE MAP OF CONNEMARA

FISSURED LIMESTONE CRAG IN THE ARAN ISLANDS

AN EXCERPT FROM THE MAP OF THE ARAN ISLANDS

geometer

DURING THE TWO years in which I was shrinking myself out of the London artworld, the works I produced became increasingly smaller and more private, dwindling finally to dots that even friends visiting my studio rarely noticed. Some of these 'points' as I called them were little round objects such as washers dropped in the gutter by people servicing their cars on Saturday afternoons, that I noticed, although not consciously looking for them, during the long abstracted country walks I used to take at that time, orienting myself by glimpses of the spires of Kilburn, Cricklewood and Neasden, or by the rumble of trains whose radial escape-routes seem to have determined the layout of the nevertheless hopelessly dull infill of late nineteenth-century housing between the crooked hearts of those onetime villages. I used to try to recover what exactly had been running through my head at the instant my eye was caught by one of these bright pavement-flowers, and sometimes back at home I would put the little disc on my index fingertip, add a drop of glue, and affix it to a wall by the act of pointing to the spot it was to occupy, so that it became what some analytic philosopher I was reading at the time calls a 'point of ostention', the point at which a line drawn from and in the direction indicted by a pointing finger first intersects a solid surface. Or I would post one off to a friend with instructions to throw it away somewhere in the house, to forget it, to find it by chance after many years, and to let me know what exactly had been the mental content of that moment of rediscovery. Although I have never received any such reflected gleams from distant con-sciousnesses, at home I did occasionally notice a visitor's gaze, idly straying across blank surfaces, suddenly arrest-ed as a reflex of sight focused attention on one of the dots I had set like traps around our rooms; then I would know that a moment had been picked up, salvaged from the blind onrush of time, that an unknown significance had arisen out of an event almost as bare and minimal as one of relativity theory's space-time data, like the curl of a questionmark from a full stop.

However, the most productive specimen of these points was one I found indoors. Lying in the bath one day I noticed a tiny yellowish smudge on the windowpane; when I stood on the lavatory seat to examine it closely it turned out to be a batch of moth-eggs — under a magni-fying glass, twenty or thirty ribbed vases tightly packed together. A few days later I noted an almost invisible activity among them; caterpillars, an eight of an inch long, were hatching out and beginning their feeding-career by eating the eggshells. I collected as many as I could on the edge of a piece of paper, and put them in an empty aquarium with a selection of leaves, among which they soon found the sort they required. These fresh minutiae of life soon grew big enough to be identified as the young of the swallow-tailed moth, a member of the family known as *Geometridae* from the earth-measuring gait of their caterpillars, which have twiglike bodies with two pairs of claspers like short soft legs at the rear, and three pairs of true legs at the front, and which progress by reaching forward as far as they can, getting a grip with the front legs and then arching the body into a loop like a cup-handle, to bring the rear close up behind the front; they are what we called 'loopers' as children, and what the Americans call inchworms. It is not the habit of loopers to let go with the claspers before having a good hold with the front legs; every move is, it seems, carefully if gropingly preconsidered, and when not walking or feeding they remain rigid and motionless, indistinguishable from twigs. But like other caterpillars they can exude a viscous substance from spinnerets on their faces that instantly dries into a silk thread and acts as a safety-line, at least when they are still small and light; sometimes in woodland glades one notices a caterpillar that has dropped from the canopy and, suddenly arrested, hangs before one's face like a little question- or exclamation-mark, before beginning to climb up again, laboriously twisting the front of its body from side to side and apparently packing the thread among its front legs.

I have always liked caterpillars; I used to breed moths and butterflies from them when I was young and living in a country town, and in London I often kept one or two of whatever species chance encounters in streets or parks had provided, in a jamjar on my studio windowledge, where they would go through their life-changes of growth and periodic skin-shedding, the torpid period of pupation, and wonderful emergence as iridescent volatilities. Sometimes in the stillness of the room — for even under the carpet of thunder the jumbo-jets labouring up from Heathrow used to unroll across the rooftops my studio was a bubble of quietude, and at night when the ambient incipient mental breakdown of the city was soothed for a while and I was waiting to be able to write or draw, it sometimes descended like a bathysphere into oceans of silence — the only sound would be the just detectable rhythmic crunch, companionable to my breathing, of a caterpillar gnawing a leaf-edge.

Only very occasionally did I witness the fabled moment of a moth's breaking out of its chrysalis; usually, even if I was keeping watch, I would find when I looked again that, on the outside of the cocoon in which the chrysalis was wrapped, there was already a dew-bedraggled tab of petals, which a few hours would then dry out and starch and iron into crisp wings ready for flight. But in fact the other transformation, from caterpillar into pupa, held more drama in its little theatre than this later one. My swallow-tails pupated in early summer, when they were about an inch and a half long. After a few days of nonstop clambering to and fro in its maze of sticks and leafstems a caterpillar would come to rest anchored by the claspers to some point from which it could just stretch its head down to the litter on the floor of the aquarium. Then it would pick up a few scraps of withered leaf one by one, and suspend them from nearby twigs and cobble them together by silken threads into a poke-shaped hammock. When all was ready, for the first time in its life it would let go completely, abandoning itself to an instant of gravity and dropping head-first into this cocoon. After a spasm of wriggling to get itself head uppermost again, and then slowly shuffling off its last caterpillar-skin to reveal the metallic-looking pupa, on which the outlines of its future wings were already faintly embossed, it would become perfectly still, and harden, and wait.

My vigils with these creatures were deeply curative for me; of what, I cannot quite say. It was during this season of the swallow-tailed moths that I made the construction I later called 'To the Centre': a slender, yard-long, white rod, suspended vertically and motionlessly in the middle of the studio by many threads of coloured silk radiating from the centre of its upper end and pulled gently taut to drawing-pins here and there in the ceiling. I believe it was also in this period that M and I formed the decision to abandon London and go to the Aran Islands to wait upon our own futures. But memory is the cocoon in which the past attends upon the invention of its significance; perhaps if I had kept a diary, or could recall posted letters, I would find that the events of that time do not cohere so appositely.

FOUR GEOMETER CATERPILLARS CONCEALED

Picture Credits:
Cover photograph, Jim Vaughan, Roundstone.
Page 12, The Irish Museum of Modern Art.
Page 20, Rijksmuseum, Amsterdam.
Pages 47 and 51, Tim Robinson.
Page 61, AD Imms *Insect Natural History* London 1947.

Designed by Colin Sackett
CORACLE, PO Box 3160, London E1 5JT